BAD DAY

by Jeni Couzyn

illustrated by
Paul Demeyer

DUTTON CHILDREN'S BOOKS • NEW YORK

CIP data is available.
First published in the United States 1990 by
Dutton Children's Books,
a division of Penguin Books USA Inc.
Originally published in Great Britain 1988 by
Victor Gollancz Ltd,
14 Henrietta Street, London WC2E 8QJ
First American Edition   Printed in Hong Kong
10 9 8 7 6 5 4 3 2 1
ISBN 0-525-44581-1

Hate this day.

Hate these toys.

Hate this food.

Hate my big brother.

Hate my little brother.

Hate my dad.

"Go away!" says Mom.

Going away.

Got my suitcase.

Got my wings.

Taking off.

Not away yet.

"Is this away?"

"No, this is the ocean."

"Is this away?"

"No, this is the city."

"Is *this* away?"

"No, my friend."

"Away isn't a place."

"Away is a feeling.

A lonely feeling."

"But there are other feelings.

Love anyone?"

"Yes. Going home!"

Love my mom, love my dad,
love my monkey, love my dog,

love my bird, love my big brother,
love my little brother, love this feeling,

love Owl.